# The Thief & His Hunter

## Book 2

BY

### Eidahs

Cover & Editing by
Binky Ink

Binky Ink

The literary arm of Binky Productions

www.binkyproductions.com/TheThiefandHisHunter

<u>WARNINGS:</u>

*Mature Subject Matter, Strong Language*

*Vomiting, Violence, Blood.*

# Table of Contents

Theron arrived at the glass casing where the quarry should have been sitting. It was empty. As Conor joined his side, Theron's eyes landed on the bloody scene at his feet.

'Oh god,' he whispered.

Conor yelped and clamped a hand to his mouth, turning away from the scene – he had never seen a dead body before.

Theron wrapped an arm around Conor in a protective embrace, bringing his face to his chest, and placed his free hand on his head, stroking his hair.

'It's okay. I'm here.'

Theron swallowed hard. He turned his face away from the scene as well.

'What's going on in there, boys?' Martha's voice came over the earpiece.

'We have a situation,' said Theron, his voice low and rough, his breath shaking.

'What kind of situation?' demanded Martha.

'Someone's taken the item and . . .' Theron exhaled through his nose, 'and replaced it with a body.'

His hold on Conor tightened and he clenched his jaw. 'Someone's trying to frame Vulpis for murder.'

<u>CHAPTER 1</u>

*Present Moment.*

Theron paced in Martha's office, seething. 'Conor's not a killer, he didn't do it.'

Conor was tight-lipped. Seeing him this upset was angering Theron even more, making him want to protect him so much more.

'I know he was up on the roofs,' Theron went on, 'but I swear, he got there at the same time as me.'

'I know. I had you in my ear the whole time. I would have recognised the sounds of a murder.' The crime scene was currently being processed by forensics, and the hypothised cause of death was a stab wound to the gut. 'Besides, I have further proof of your location, Conor.'

'Martha?' warned Theron. He didn't like what her tone was alluding to. 'What have you omitted to tell us?'

'I've been tracking Conor.' Martha raised her hands in defence as Theron opened his mouth to interject. 'It was part of the deal I made with *my* superiors.'

'Uh, sorry, but Conor never takes his phone with him,' said Theron.

'Never said it was his phone.'

Conor pulled his hood back, checking it.

'The hood, isn't it?' concluded Theron, pointing a thumb at the garment.

'And it's a good thing I did.' Martha folded her arms. 'With Conor on probation, he needs all the evidence on his side.'

'Yeah, well, you call me when the forensics have more evidence.' Theron took Conor by the hand and began leading him out of the office.

'And where are you going?'

Theron stopped, looking over his shoulder. 'Home. Where it's safe.'

Theron led Conor to the car, muttering angrily to himself. 'I'm sorry,' he said more softly before starting the vehicle. 'I don't want you to think I'm angry at you. None of this is your fault, darling.'

Conor didn't answer. His silence was worrying.

When they stepped through the door of the penthouse, Conor clamped a gloved hand to his mouth, tears pouring down his face.

'Hey, darling,' Theron placed his hand on Conor's back. 'It's okay.' He began to wrap his arms around him, but Conor squirmed out of the embrace and ran straight to the bathroom, where he bent over the toilet and vomited.

Theron was a bit relieved. With that out, maybe Conor would be able to talk.

Theron joined Conor in the bathroom, sitting on the tiles, where Conor let himself plop down beside him, breathing heavily. Both of them leaned their heads against the wall.

'It's a shock. It always is.' Theron paused.

Conor wiped his mouth with the back of his hand. Fidelis skittered towards them and rested her muzzle at Conor's feet. Theron reached towards the dog and scratched her head.

'I puked too the first time I saw a body. Except I didn't wait till I got home – I literally puked *on* the body.'

That got a chuckle out of Conor.

'Barry was livid. I'd never seen him so angry.' Theron imitated the old man's voice and accent. 'Tampering with the evidence.' Theron laughed, then resumed in his normal voice. 'Then he reassured me. Told me I can always look away. And I do. Every time.'

'Do you see a lot of bodies?' asked Conor, his eyes on Fidelis.

Theron smiled softly, heartened that Conor had spoken.

'No. It's rare. I am not from that division. But it does happen. This one time, I even found the killer standing over the body. The chase led me to a haunted house.' Theron frowned. 'Killer got away.' He sighed.

'One time, the only time for this exception, I caused one. I killed in the line of duty. It haunted me for months.'

After a few heartbeats, Conor asked, 'What happened?'

'Perpetrator had his gun on Barry – he wasn't backing down. Barry had been disarmed. The perpetrator twitched.

I shot.' Theron passed a hand over his face. 'It was the only time I shot to kill. I always shoot to injure.' He paused. 'Barry said I made the right call.'

'He's probably right.' Conor kept looking down at Fidelis. 'Would you have shot *me*?'

'God, no. That first encounter, before I even knew you were the thief I was hunting? I just wanted Vulpis to *think* I would shoot him. Darling,' Theron took Conor's hand and interlaced their fingers. He looked at Conor who finally met his gaze. 'Someone's after you. I am so angry, so . . . scared. I will not let anything happen to you. I'm going to protect you with my life.'

Conor's eyes brimmed with fresh tears. He whispered, 'Don't die for me.'

Theron pulled him into his arms as a sob escaped each of them. 'I promise.'

They held each other tightly. After a time, they moved to lie down on the bed over the blankets, weeping until they both fell asleep.

* * *

When Conor woke up, Theron was no longer in bed. Conor had felt comforted by his arms around him. Now, he needed that comfort once more, even if the memory of his fiancé's strong arms holding him continued to mildly reassure him.

He heard voices coming from the kitchen, one of them baritone. Dragging himself out of bed, and setting his puke-smelling convertible leather gloves aside as he changed into something more casual, Conor joined Theron and their guest.

An older man sat with Theron – he was perhaps in his sixties. His white hair was speckled with remnants of blond, and his eyes curled into a permanent smile as he beamed at Theron.

The man stood and immediately offered his hand to Conor. 'Howdie! Name's Barry. Barry Weisner. Shall I call you Vulpis or Conor?' He spoke with a mild Texan accent.

'Uh, Conor's fine.'

The man clasped both hands on Conor's. 'Wonderful. I've never seen Theron so happy and loved up if I'm honest.'

Conor couldn't help but smile as Theron blushed.

'Barry.' Theron's warning was as much chiding as it was embarrassment.

'It's true. Theron tells me you keep each other on your toes. Sign of a healthy relationship, that.'

As Barry turned away, Conor mouthed, 'Can we trust him?'

'Yes,' Theron mouthed back.

'Now, I brought the files you asked about.' Barry pulled out a large binder.

'Whoa,' voiced Conor.

'I asked Barry to dig up anything he could about Vulpis jobs,' explained Theron.

Conor finally pulled out a chair and sat down. 'Right.' He clasped his hands together. 'I don't even remember all my jobs.'

'I wasn't supposed to have this on hand. Martha kept chiding me whenever she discovered me "digging uselessly," as she called it.' Barry made air quotes and imitated Martha's tone when he said it. He chuckled. 'I reckon it was premonition . . . for now.'

Barry opened the binder. 'I'd been tracking the items stolen by Vulpis, and monitored the locations. If anything stands out, if anyone has it in for Vulpis, it'll be in here. Except I can't cross-reference anything in the system.' He paused deliberately. 'But *you* can.'

Theron began to thank Barry when his phone chimed. He brought the phone to his ear. He answered with that same terseness he always did. 'Theron Morin. . . . Martha, what do you have?' He scowled. 'What do you mean no fingerprints? . . . Then cross-reference *outside* of CODIS.'

Theron hung up. He let out a slow breath, working his jaw. 'Our perpetrator has no fingerprints.' He pointed at the binder. 'Got any ideas, Barry?'

'Actually, yeh. It was pretty huge.' Barry began sifting through the binder. 'Pawnshop just outside of town, the day after Vulpis took a watch from there.'

'I remember reading up on that,' said Conor, pressing a hand on his chest in attempt to quell his thumping heart. 'It's disturbing. We had receipts, that watch was stolen, and my client even went to the police and the pawnshop owner, and *no one* wanted to help her.' Conor lowered his voice as the mere memory clenched his heart. 'I felt guilty it all might've been my fault. I stopped taking jobs for a while after that.'

'What happened?' Theron's brows were creased in concern.

'Ah, here we are.' Barry pointed at the page.

Theron began reading the details, using his finger to track his place on the page.

'There was a hostage situation at that shop,' explained Barry. 'A SWAT team had to go in.' Barry became grave. 'A bomb went off. As far as anyone knows, only the SWAT team leader survived.'

Theron's eyes narrowed, his finger on a name, and his face contorted in rage as he growled, 'I can't believe it.'

'Babe?'

'L. Sanchez.'

'Who's L. Sanchez?'

'Lorenzo,' seethed Theron, balling his hands into fists. 'He shot you that night.' Theron clenched his jaw, speaking through his teeth. 'I'm going to fucking kill him.'

CHAPTER 2

Theron marched through the halls at H.Q. 'Where the fuck is he?' he growled under his breath. He was seeing red.

'Babe,' Conor called out, keeping pace just a step behind him, 'let's be smart about this.'

'Smart about what?' Martha joined them, matching Theron's strides.

'Lorenzo's linked to a past Vulpis job and might want to exact revenge.'

'Lorenzo has fingerprints,' Martha reminded him as Theron veered around a corner.

'I don't care!'

Martha gave Theron a warning look.

'He shot Conor when I never gave the order to. Plus that past job? That makes him my number one suspect on my list.'

Theron saw his quarry in the locker room. He ran the rest of the way and, grabbing Lorenzo by the collar, shoved him against the lockers.

'You got something you wanna tell us, Lorenzo? Like maybe your SWAT team died after a Vulpis job and you might want revenge?'

'Get your hands off me!' Lorenzo easily shoved Theron against the opposite locker. He was bigger than Theron, his muscles much more pronounced, and he was taller, but that didn't intimidate Theron. He knew he was strong enough to take him on if he had to.

'Time out, both of you!' Martha shouted.

'You pulled the trigger on Conor!' shouted Theron.

'Off, now!' Martha stepped in between them, and with one hand on each of their sternums, shoved them against an opposite locker and held them in place. Lorenzo tried to move away, as did Theron, who tried to grapple at Lorenzo. Martha's hold on them prevented them from doing any of that.

Conor blinked. 'Damn, you're strong.'

'Gotta be. With people under my supervision who don't behave. Come on!'

'You shot Conor!' screamed Theron, his voice cracking, his heart breaking.

'Yeah, I made the wrong call. Sue me.'

'Oh, I just might.'

'Gentlemen. If you don't start behaving right now, I'm going to put you both on leave of absence.'

Theron lifted his hands in surrender. 'Fine.'

Martha backed away, letting go of the two men.

'I made the wrong call, okay!?' Lorenzo spat. 'But I shot to injure. I never miss my shots.'

'Thanks, I guess?' voiced Conor.

'You wanna know what happened with the SWAT team, huh?' Lorenzo shouted at Theron, taking a step towards him and getting in his space again.

Theron leaned forward menacingly. 'Enlighten me.'

'Vulpis's client wasn't the only one after that watch. Yeah, it belonged to his client, but mobsters wanted in on it, and some dirty cop arranged the deal so they'd get it.'

'That explains no one helping my client,' muttered Conor.

'That hostage situation . . . I was the only one far enough from the blast. We didn't know there was a bomb. I sent my team in.' Lorenzo seethed in Theron's face, speaking through his gritting teeth. 'That explosion saw my wife dead.'

Theron swallowed hard. He didn't know what he'd do if he lost Conor.

Lorenzo backed away. 'Do me one thing, eh? Never take each other for granted.' He marched out of the room.

Theron bowed his head.

'I swear to god, Theron, one more outburst from you and I *will* put you on leave of absence.'

Martha spun on her heels. Theron grabbed her arm, pulling her back but maintaining a loose grip so she'd know this was urgent and not a threat.

'Something doesn't add up, Martha. All of Vulpis's jobs go through us now, they're documented. So how did the perpetrator know?'

Martha pursed her lips. 'Then the next one, we leave off the record.'

* * *

The time came for the next job. Conor was nervous as hell. He had Theron by his side to protect him if anything went awry. Thankfully, it went without a hitch, as did the next one.

'I trust him less and less,' Theron had complained about Lorenzo.

Conor was in the locker room now, while Theron was in a meeting with Martha. Conor was finally starting to relax again on jobs.

'Hey Vulpis!'

Conor froze. He looked over his shoulder at Lorenzo who was hulking towards him.

'Bold of you to be alone when there's someone here you don't trust.'

Conor turned to face the other man, heart thumping in his chest. 'You don't scare me.'

Lorenzo chuckled mirthlessly. 'You're a bad liar, Vulpis.'

Conor swallowed hard and reflexively took a step back. Within seconds, Lorenzo was on top of him, shoving him against a locker, pinning him with his arms and an elbow pressed against his chest, a knee locking him in place. Lorenzo seethed in Conor's face.

'What do you want, Lorenzo?'

'What do I want?' Lorenzo arched his eyebrows. 'I want a lot of things. I want to trust my gut without question, I want my wife alive. But those are two things I don't think I'll ever have again.'

'I'm sorry about your wife,' said Conor, his voice a feeble half-whisper.

'What's that? I didn't quite hear you?'

'I'm sorry about your wife,' Conor said more forcefully. Tears stung his eyes. 'Look, I really am.'

'So you admit it's your fault?'

Conor shook his head. It had taken him months to get over it, but like Theron, Barry, and Martha had told him, it wasn't his fault dirty cops were involved with the mafia for a stupid watch someone else had stolen from someone unrelated to either of them.

'I advise you to watch your step, Vulpis.' Lorenzo pulled out his gun and pressed the muzzle to Conor's chin.

Conor gulped. He'd never felt more scared in his entire life. 'Are you going to kill me?'

Lorenzo snickered and smirked menacingly. He spoke through his teeth. 'If I wanted to kill you, Vulpis, I would already have done so. Just remember that I don't miss.'

Lorenzo pressed the muzzle a little harder before holstering the pistol, just to stress his point. Conor tried to shove Lorenzo off him but the bigger man prevented him from moving.

'We're not done here.'

Conor winced trying to turn his face away. Lorenzo grabbed him by the chin, squeezing hard and forcing him to look at him.

'I've got my eye on you, Vulpis. Try *anything* . . . and it'll be the last thing you do. Got it?'

Conor merely nodded.

'Oh, and if you breathe a word about this to any-one, and I mean *anyone*, then I'll just have to tell your loverboy you and I had an intimate exchange.'

Someone pulled Lorenzo off Conor, shoving him against the opposite locker so hard the clunk echoed in the room.

'Keep your hands to yourself, Lorenzo!' growled Theron. 'Conor and I have no secrets.'

Lorenzo pushed Theron off him, fixing his collar. 'You think your partner's righteous? That he helps people? How many dirty secrets does he have? How many jobs did he do for lowlives who are just like him? How many times did one of his jobs put someone else at risk? You can't trust people like that, Theron.'

Lorenzo marched out of the locker room. Theron turned to Conor. 'Darling, are you okay?'

Conor lunged forward, wrapping his arms around Theron as a sob escaped him. 'He had his gun on me.'

*'He what?'*

Conor was overcome by a fit of the shakes. He held Theron more tightly.

'Just so you know, nothing anyone can say will *ever* make me not trust you, Conor.' Theron's voice was soothing, but Conor could hear the strain in it from the anger he was undoubtedly feeling. 'You're the love of my life. I trust you with my life.'

Theron tightened his hold too. The protective squeeze helped calm Conor somewhat.

Theron then led Conor by the hand to Martha's office, his face contorted in rage.

'Lorenzo just threatened my fiancé at gunpoint.'

Martha's face reflected Theron's anger. She took her phone and brought it to her ear. 'Lorenzo, my office. Now!' As soon as Lorenzo arrived, she narrowed her eyes. 'I'm putting you on forced leave of absence. Effective immediately. Badge and gun on my desk.'

Seething, Lorenzo obliged before walking out and slamming the door to Martha's office so hard that it shook.

'Are you still okay for tonight's job, Conor?'

Conor nodded. He put a hand to his chest to further calm his nerves. 'It's a standard job.'

The job was in a club. One of the bartenders was supposed to deliver the item to Vulpis. Except something felt off.

'Why can't the bartender deliver this item directly to your client?' muttered Theron.

Conor ensured to maintain a low level as his eyes scanned the club. 'I never ask. Typically it's because they can't be seen together.'

'And what if this forces you to break the law?' Theron's brows were knit together in concern.

'Babe, we ran it through the system. I even told my client this exchange had to be above-board.'

'You telling them it has to be above-board doesn't mean it is.'

Conor squeezed Theron's hand, trying to convey his reassurance, even if he too was worried. Having Martha in his ear wasn't doing anything to assuage the anxiety. Knowing she was right outside the club, however, did.

'Darling, we don't know where that figurine has been.'

Conor suppressed a laugh. Theron rolled his eyes, probably realising the sense of the sentence. It alleviated *some* anxiety at least.

'Babe, this statuette? I've delivered tons like it. I once had to deliver a mannequin doll, okay? This item isn't a problem.'

Theron's eyes widened. 'Life-size? What the!' He shook his head, following Conor deeper into the club as the thief led him by the hand.

Conor approached the bar. An older woman with a pleasant smile was wiping the counter.

'Hi, I'm looking for Johanne.'

'She's on break, honey. You can find her on the roof . . . if you can scale up there.'

'Thanks.' Conor chuckled. 'Happens I'm an expert with roofs.'

The bartender perked up. 'You good fixing a leaking roof gutter, then?'

Conor hesitated, 'Uh, I'll get back to you on that.' He winked before leaving the bar.

Conor and Theron made their way to the roof. The night air was crisp and few leaves remained on their trees; the branches swayed ominously with the wind, reinforcing the unease Conor felt in his gut.

A slender woman stood with her back to them. Even out here, it was brighter than the dimness of the club.

'Johanne?' Conor asked.

The woman laughed, her cackle high-pitched – it sounded condescending. 'I can't believe you took my bait, Vulpis.'

A rock formed in the pit of Conor's stomach. Theron's hand twitched closer to his gun.

The woman slowly turned around, and Conor glimpsed the burn scar all across her face and neck.

Theron unholstered his gun and trained it on her, the movement so fast, it barely took two seconds. The detective held the gun steadily with both hands, his jaw clenched, his gaze ablaze with the protectiveness he had always displayed for Conor.

Through his earpiece, Conor heard Martha barking orders to her squad and running to join the scene.

'It's you,' concluded Conor. 'You're the one trying to frame me.'

'Very good, Vulpis. I was also the anonymous tip the night you got shot. I was trying to corner you, but *he* – Johanne shot Theron a vehement glare – 'and his squad was in my way and hunting you – I had to hide.'

She pouted, her voice complaintive, on top of condescending. 'And then you two were always together, so I resorted to other means to try to corner you.' Now her tone grew cold, as did her eyes. 'Except since that didn't work, *this* time . . .' Conor felt like his heart had stopped, seeing Johanne produce a long dagger. 'I'm here to kill you.'

Theron shot, but Johanne somersaulted with expert ease.

'Get behind me.' Theron stepped in front of Conor. 'Not another step, Johanne.'

'Who?' She giggled with condescension. 'That's just a name. Not mine.'

Johanne – or whatever her name was – leapt into the air, landing behind Conor. She wrapped her arm around his neck, pulling him away from Theron and pressing the dagger against his throat.

Conor felt like his heart was going to beat out of his chest, and his legs were shaking and weak.

Theron spun, pulling back the safety of his gun. 'Let him go! I won't ask you again.' His hands were trembling now, and Conor could see the fear in his hunter's eyes. Conor trusted him to take the shot he needed to.

Johanne hum-chuckled in glee. 'I have Vulpis now.' She tightened her grip, but her focus made the dagger arm move lower to Conor's sternum. 'What do you have to say for yourselves now?'

'Fifth grade, the incident with the trash cans,' was all Theron said.

Conor knew what he meant. They had fallen off some trash cans in opposite directions to throw their pursuers off. One of Conor's less ideal reckless moments, and as per, he had dragged Theron into it with him. They still walked out of there with bags of ramen. Conor hoped they'd be able to joke about that later, over some ramen.

Theron blinked three times, as he had back then. Then Conor put all his weight to his left, trusting the dagger was low enough it wouldn't graze him.

Theron shot, getting their perpetrator in the arm – her right arm. She screamed, backing away from Conor and clutching her bleeding arm.

Shouting in gruff anger, she ran forward, right at Theron, and jumped onto a low chimney to leap over him just as he shot, missing her completely. She landed right on top of him.

Conor watched in horror as her dagger struck true through his back, protruding and bloody from the front of Theron's ribs – Theron, who stared out, wide-eyed.

'THERON!' screamed Conor.

Johanne retracted the dagger from Theron's back and began bounding away.

Conor ran to Theron, who dropped his gun and crumpled to the ground. Tears blurring his vision, Conor took hold of Theron's gun with both hands and shot again and again at their perpetrator until she had leapt out of view.

Discarding the gun, Conor fell to his knees, the scrape dull compared to the agony in his shattering heart. It was more pain than he had ever been in. Conor cradled Theron as his lover's blood drenched his clothes. Theron's eyes met Conor's before they fell shut and his body went limp.

Conor wailed his heartache.

Martha arrived on the scene. 'Medic! We need a medic *now!*' She wrapped something around Theron's abdomen.

Conor was gasping and heaving, rocking Theron as he hunched over him, his tears falling on him.

Conor's chest was tight, he couldn't breathe. He let out another wail.

A firm hand gripped his. 'He's going to survive. I've seen people survive worse.'

Conor let Martha lead him as medics placed Theron onto a gurney and wheeled him into an ambulance. Conor stayed with Theron, while Martha followed close behind in her car.

After bandaging Theron to contain the bleeding, the medics cleaned Conor's hands from Theron's blood and checked Conor for injuries during the ride.

Aside from the blood all over Theron's clothes, Theron looked like he was sleeping, his face relaxed. Conor was uncertain if that meant something good or if it meant something bad.

When they arrived at the hospital, the medics pushed Theron on the gurney through to the E.R. and something started beeping. Conor overheard, 'Critical condition.'

Conor put the back of his hand to his mouth, face pained in anguish. 'Fifteen years apart. Nothing will make up for it. He has to survive, Martha. I've loved him since we were five.'

'I know.' Martha wrapped an arm around Conor who collapsed in her embrace. The woman was strong, and she supported his weight, leading him to some chairs, where they sat down and waited.

Eventually, Conor calmed. Barry arrived – Martha must've contacted him on her way to the hospital – and Conor stood before collapsing again on his chair.

'Have you eaten anything, kid?'

'I'm not hungry.' Conor shook his head. 'I don't know if I had Lorenzo pegged wrong, but he knew nothing about tonight.'

'They already tracked down this Johanne's home,' said Martha. 'It's a makeshift. And there were no Johannes in that blast.'

'Her face,' Conor wept angrily. 'She survived the explosion.' He scrunched up his face. 'And she's good at parkour.'

'We'll use that, and—'

A doctor approached them. Conor stood, forcing himself to remain upright.

'We've managed to stabilise him.'

'Oh, thank god,' breathed Conor, bringing a hand to his mouth.

'Except his left kidney was severely damaged and the right was punctured.'

Conor felt sick.

'The angle of the stab wound through his flank thankfully didn't touch any other vital organ,' the doctor went on, 'but with both kidneys compromised, your partner could face dialysis and could be unable to continue his duties as a detective, not to mention face complications.'

Conor didn't understand half those words, but he knew it was bad.

'If he's to survive and function . . . he's going to need a kidney transplant.'

A loud sob escaped Conor. He felt like he was about to have another fit of the shakes or pass out. He couldn't process this, process losing Theron or—

Barry stepped forth. 'I'll do it.' Conor stared at the old man. Barry stood resolute. 'I have no use for two now anyway. I'm healthy, and Theron and I have the same blood type.'

'We'll need to undergo a series of tests,' the doctor acknowledged. 'If you'll follow me.'

Conor slowly sank back down as his vision blurred ever more, convinced he would collapse at any moment.

'You see, he's in good hands. He'll get through this.' Martha, sitting on the chair beside him, rubbed his back. It did little to comfort him.

'If he dies,' whispered Conor, 'my life is over.'

# Chapter 4

The rest was a haze. Barry going into the O.R., both Barry and Theron being brought to a room, Martha leaving the hospital.

Conor held Theron's hand, pleading for him to be okay. He looked so peaceful, and Conor just wanted to see him twitch, something – anything – to tell him he was going to be okay.

Barry, who had already awakened, kept reassuring him and reiterating what the doctor had said, but Conor wouldn't be reassured until Theron regained consciousness.

Conor held Theron's hand near his mouth, resting his head on Theron's thigh. Theron's fingers moved. Conor's head shot up as Theron groaned, opening his eyes.

Conor lunged for Theron's lips, pressing a hard and desperate kiss that he hoped conveyed all his love and devotion. Theron moaned, placing a hand on Conor's side. The touch elicited a wave of emotions and Conor wept into the kiss, his eyes shut tight as tears wet both their faces.

Theron deepened the kiss, thrusting his tongue and opening his mouth before slightly pulling away. 'Is this the afterlife? If so, it's rather arousing.'

Conor let out a half-laugh, half sob. 'You're alive. Theron, babe, my love, you're alive!'

Conor put a hand to Theron's face, as the other man cupped Conor's cheek. 'It appears I am.'

'I was so scared I'd lose you,' Conor wept.

'They'll have to try a lot harder before they take me away from you.' Theron reassured. He winced. 'Looks like they patched me up good.'

'You needed a transplant.' Conor looked over at the other bed – Theron's eyes widened when he followed his gaze, tears brimming his eyes.

'Barry.'

'Only for my kiddo partner.' Barry's smile was warm. 'Always considered you like a son. Couldn't have any of my own, infertility and whatnot, but you, you were the one I looked out for.'

Theron pressed his lips together as tears streamed down his face. He whispered, 'Thank you.'

Conor was finally able to feel the relief he had sought, even while his heart continued to clench and unclench. He and Theron wrapped their arms around each other as best they could without aggravating the injury, and Theron dosed back to sleep.

Conor returned home to get cleaned and changed. As soon as he arrived, he leaned against the door and slid to the floor. Fidelis scurried to him and he wrapped his arms around her tightly, breaking down in tears.

* * *

When Theron opened his eyes, Conor was no longer there. His eyes darted this way and that as his heart thudded in his chest.

'Relax, kid,' came the soothing baritone voice from the bed beside Theron's. 'He went to get some things from home.'

Theron remembered Barry and what he'd done for him, and was reassured.

The doctor checked up on Theron and explained a few things. Then Theron and Barry chatted until Conor returned. The thief had changed, but his face was streaked with tears.

Theron reached a hand up to him. 'Darling,' he said softly.

Conor heaved. 'If I'd never been able to hear you call me that again . . .' Conor sat down on the edge of the bed, his lips pressed together as he held back his tears.

'Hey, it's okay.' Theron took Conor's hand and brushed a soft kiss to it. He couldn't help his curiosity. 'Any new info on this Johanne character?'

Conor shook his head. 'Not her real name. Martha managed to get some I.D. on a survivor who must be her, but no leads. And we still don't know what Lorenzo's game is.' Conor's grip on Theron's hand tightened. 'If they're working together or not.'

'Darling, you're squeezing my fingers,' Theron warned gently.

Conor immediately loosened his grip. 'Sorry.'

'We'll get to the bottom of this. I promise.'

'You also promised you wouldn't die for me,' Conor retorted in anger.

Theron cupped Conor's cheek. 'I haven't. And I won't. I don't ever intend on breaking that promise.'

* * *

Conor now stood in Martha's office, which felt smaller today. Martha had a stern gaze. She stood directly in front of him, her arms crossed.

She had called him in, tearing him away from his fiancé's side. It had barely been a couple of days and already she had important business to discuss with him – or so she had said.

'I've made an executive decision and just received the O.K. from my superiors. The other night, you used Theron's gun to shoot at the assassin.'

Conor's chest clenched at the mention. She was no longer a perpetrator, but an *assassin*.

Martha's tone became one of scolding. 'And you missed *every single time*. What were you thinking? You don't have the training for it, you could have hurt yourself!' She sighed. 'I'm going to get you the proper gun training. Looks like you need it.'

Conor twisted his mouth in disdain. 'I wish I hadn't missed.'

Martha grabbed Conor by the arms. 'You're not a killer, Conor.'

'I wish I were,' he seethed. 'I want to end her.'

'I'm going to dismiss that. I'm going to train you so you can protect yourself and your man, got it?'

# Chapter 5

Under Martha's tutelage, Conor began his training with a gun, shooting stationary and moving targets alike. He was quick to pick up the skill, and his rage towards the woman who nearly took his future husband from him kept him focused.

Conor felt powerful, wielding a pistol. Never did he think he would ever carry such a weapon, though his steeled state made him want it now, he realised – to protect Theron.

Despite having moved away from the hometown where they grew up together, and then after moving around a bit, Conor somehow still wound up in the same city as Theron, as though they were meant to be. He'd be damned if he let anything happen to him, and his desire to equally protect his hunter, just as his hunter would protect him, fuelled Conor all the more.

Martha also trained Conor in more combat tactics. He already knew self-defence, which he needed just for being Vulpis, so these techniques complemented that well.

Martha was a strict teacher, pouring her many years of experience into her discipline. No wonder Theron was terse when he was at work. Conor admired Martha, even if she was a bit scary at times. She had earned her place as the Chief Investigator of the Investigative Department of Police. Her presence demanded respect without her uttering a single word. Martha certainly had Conor's respect.

Coupled with the care she showed Conor and Theron, and the scrutiny she had put into finding a solution so Conor would not go to prison, it made her someone Conor felt he could trust with his life – and with Theron's life.

Autumn turned to winter, and Theron came home. Barry came to stay with them. The two recovering men would be able to help each other, not to mention keep each other company when Conor was out, and Conor would be able to help them both. Besides, Fidelis had taken quite a liking to the old man.

Conor had just finished putting on his Vulpis leathers when he heard his lover's angry tone behind him.

'What is the meaning of this?'

Conor sighed, turning to face Theron.

'You're doing a job without me?'

'I did jobs without you for over ten years, Theron,' Conor retorted.

'But you didn't have an assassin hunting you back then!' protested Theron. His voice grew dangerous again. 'She never even went to a hospital for that bullet I put in her arm. She either knows people on the black market or can take care of herself more than we thought. If she lays another hand on you, Conor, I swear . . .'

Conor tried to make Theron smile, and teased, 'You'll lose your shit?'

'I'm losing my shit now!' cried Theron. 'Please, Conor, I'm begging you. Don't go!'

Conor closed the distance between them and cupped Theron's face with both hands. 'I am not leaving you and you are not losing me. I promise you that. But Vulpis needs to continue his work, if not to pay rent, to lure our assassin out.'

Tears brimmed Theron's eyes. It tugged at Conor's heart, it always did. Their love could be so intense, it had always been, even as kids and teens, any little fight had either or both of them crying like babies before they reconciled.

The assassin, whether working independently or not, had by now been identified as Marie Adoncourt. She had survived the blast, and spent months in hospital recovering from the burns. Now she had gone underground. Everyone was searching for her but nothing was popping up.

Theron lowered his gaze and his eyes widened. 'Is that a gun at your belt?!'

Conor sighed – he had not yet told Theron about his drills. 'Martha's training me. She got the okay. This is legit.'

Theron backed away, hand on his mouth. 'It's not even safe enough for you to be out there without a gun and you expect me *not* to freak out?'

'I'll be fine.' Conor began out of the room.

Theron grabbed him by the arm, spinning him back around. 'No! I won't let you go. I implore you, Conor. You're not doing this job.'

Conor had never heard Theron so commanding before, not in all their years of knowing each other. He knew this meant Theron was frightened beyond measure. It staggered Conor's heart and clenched his chest to know his fiancé felt this desperate.

Conor softened his eyes and tone. 'I have to go. I will be safe.'

He stepped out of the room and towards his balcony.

'I'll stop you! Or go with you!' Theron ran towards him, arm outstretched, and then winced and cried out gruffly, stopping short and stumbling to lean against the wall, pressing on the side of his abdomen.

Conor ran to him. 'Babe! You're recovering from an injury *and* surgery. You could have died! Let your body heal.' Conor steadied him with both hands.

Theron's response was rough. 'If you expect me to be the stay-at-home husband once we're married, while you go out gallivanting, then you'll be sorely disappointed.' Theron's face contorted, nose crinkling. 'Our marriage won't work.'

That hit Conor in the gut. 'Don't you dare start that again, a fight for no reason,' he seethed. 'This is what you do when you don't want to lose me. And the last time I believed your words of anger and hatred, we spent fifteen years apart. Our marriage *will* work because we've moved past that.' Conor clenched his jaw. 'I want to retort that it won't work if you keep poking me and hurting me like that, but I'm reckless,' he raised his voice, 'and I'm marrying you no matter what!'

Theron's eyes widened. He threw his arms around Conor, holding him so tightly, his fear made Conor fear.

'Babe,' Conor reassured.

'My darling,' whispered Theron. He kissed Conor's neck. 'I don't know what I'd do without you.'

'Then stop alluding to a future where our marriage won't work. It's so hurtful.'

'I'm sorry.' Theron pulled away enough to stare into Conor's eyes. 'I'm sorry, you don't deserve that.' Theron squeezed his eyes shut and a tear trickled down his cheek. Conor wiped it away gently with his thumb.

'You do realise it's reckless to do that, right?' Conor pointed out.

They both let out soft chuckles.

Conor sighed. 'Come, let's get you settled into the living room.'

'I *can* walk on my own, you know.'

'Says the man who slammed into the wall from the pain of running towards me.'

'With my arm up,' Theron defended. 'Must've stretched my healing scar.'

Conor reflexively lifted Theron's shirt and took the time to check the two bandage, front and back – all was fine. He helped Theron sit on the sofa beside Barry, who was reading a magazine and doing a good job of looking like he was minding his own business.

Without lifting his eyes from the article he was reading, he voiced, 'How 'bout a compromise?'

Conor and Theron looked at the old man, both waiting for him to elaborate.

'You both have phones. Text messaging, I hear, is the modern way of communicating.' He chuckled. 'Unless Conor wants to *fax* in he's safe.'

The thought made Conor laugh. 'But I never bring my phone with me . . . Oh!' He grinned.

* * *

'Darling?' Theron was uncertain. He had just nearly opened up his stitches, just nearly caused another cosmic fight between him and Conor, just nearly let his fear control him all over again.

Still grinning widely, Conor brought a hand to his ear. 'Hey Martha, I have a favour to ask you.'

It felt as though a huge pressure had been lifted from Theron's chest. Conor placed his hands on Theron's knees, bending and leaning in.

'I love you,' he mouthed. He kissed Theron, not too quick but not long enough for Theron's liking, before backing away to the balcony.

Conor blew Theron another kiss and winked before jumping up and swinging himself onto the roof.

'You know, he's right that it's reckless to stir the pot like that,' said Barry, turning to Theron.

'You heard everything, didn't you?'

'Every single word.' Barry sighed. 'That man loves you like no other has loved you. You're both crazy for each other. If you poke and poke and poke, you'll hurt him. You have to express your fear instead.'

'I know.'

'And that devotion! Even if you hurt him, wanting to be with you. He's a keeper, kiddo.'

'Kiddo. As though I'm five.'

'Oh, like you didn't just act like a five-year-old just now!'

'Stop,' laughed Theron. The vibration of the laugh tickled his healing wounds.

A text message came through to Theron from Martha. *Conor is on approach to destination. All is well so far.* Then another message came in a few minutes later. *You're going to have to get over this fear of yours, Theron. I will not babysit you forever.*

Theron chuckled, and showed Barry the messages. Barry arched a brow, making a face that said 'She's right.'

The two men busied themselves with Fidelis and crosswords. Barry went to bed in the guest bedroom. Theron remained in the living room, receiving texts from Martha from time to time. Eventually, he fell asleep before a thud jolted him awake.

Theron lifted his head to find Conor standing on the balcony as he entered the penthouse, sliding the glass door quietly but quickly. Conor strode straight to Theron and gave him a fiery and reassuring kiss that tightened his stomach elatedly. Theron felt like he could breathe again, now that Conor was home.

# CHAPTER 6

The weeks passed, winter was underway, and Theron's and Barry's healing showed great promise. Their stitches were out now but they had to be careful. Such surgery took time to fully heal and for no pain to resurge. Theron's activities would be subdued and minimised for another good while.

Conor was in the locker room with some of the other detectives, teasing each other.

'Come on, you can't possibly tell me you haven't once had sex since Theron returned from the hospital. Pe-lease. There are ways to get creative.' She winked.

'Surely he's good for it now, no?' one of the guys pressed.

Conor chuckled. It *had* been a couple of months, and he *did* crave his fiancé, but he'd respect Theron's needs. 'Instead of focusing on *my* sex life, maybe you should focus on *yours*.' He winked.

'Ooooh.' The others echoed as a chorus.

'Touché. Look, I just don't know anymore how to be romantic.'

'Then don't try to be romantic, man. Just tell your wife you desire her. As for me, Theron hasn't expressed anything and I want to respect his recovery speed.'

Conor turned – and froze when he saw Lorenzo stepping into the locker room.

'Because this isn't familiar,' Conor muttered under his breath.

Fuming, he marched to Martha's office and slammed the door behind him. Then he slammed his hands down on her desk. 'Can you tell me what the fuck Lorenzo is doing here?'

Martha stood from her seat, calm as ever, and came to stand before Conor who pushed away from the desk.

She muttered. 'The way you agents talk to me some-times . . . And *I'm* the superior.' She met Conor's steely gaze, her tone now all-business. 'We don't know that Lorenzo was ever trying to target you. The media has been talking Vulpis up to lure your assassin out, but we just don't know when she'll strike again.'

'So you chose to bring in another threat instead?' demanded Conor.

Martha's expression became grave and she pressed her lips in a straight line, her eyes never leaving Conor's. He found himself mimicking the expression.

'Vulpis,' she said, her voice low. 'Are you ready to be reckless?'

'Yes, ma'am.'

* * *

Theron watched as Barry did some wall push-ups. 'I swear, you heal faster than me. I lift my arm and I still feel a pull.'

'I feel a pull, but exercise will help the rest heal even faster.'

Theron sighed. 'I don't know why Conor has to spend so many hours at the office.'

'Maybe it has to do with his probation?' Barry reminded him.

'Yeah.' Theron felt a tug in his heart. 'I miss him. I always do when we're not in the same room.' Hugging a pillow and pouting, he grabbed the remote and turned the T.V. on.

'Illusive thief on remand, Vulpis,' – Theron leaned forward in his seat, Barry stopped what he was doing – 'has issued a challenge to the assassin attempting to kill him. Earlier today, he went live with these words.'

On the screen, Conor appeared in full Vulpis attire, his face barely visible. Theron held his breath.

'You and me, Marie, the first location where we met face-to-face. Tonight. I will be alone. It's time to hash things out once and for all.'

The reporter continued, 'One can only hope that the sly fox has something up his sleeve.'

'I know where that is.' Theron closed the T.V. and jumped up, dashing for the door. 'It's not too late. If we get to H.Q. on time, we might be able to stop him.'

'Oh, now you're dragging *me* into this?'

Theron glanced back, pleading. 'Barry, I'm scared, okay?'

'I'm with you, son.'

The two hobbled out the door. Theron nearly missed a step running down the stairs, he was going so fast. Barry steadied him.

'Careful,' he chided. 'You're no use to your man if you injure yourself again.'

Theron ignored the comment, and when they entered the car, he pressed on the gas. Willing the traffic to move faster, Theron nearly missed a few stops and ran several red lights.

He bolted into the office, looking for Conor.

'Conor!'

He ran to his office. Empty.

He ran to Martha's office. Empty.

'Theron, good to see you.' Theron spun around. 'If you're looking for Conor or Martha, they left already.'

'No, no, no!'

'It'll be fine, they've got backup. Hey, did you know Lorenzo's back?'

'What?' Theron's voice was nearly a threat and his emphasis on the *T* made that clear.

'He's fine now, so no worries.'

The detective walked away.

Theron turned back to find papers strewn about on Martha's desk. There was an open file with the address of the club whose roof upon which they had encountered the assassin. Theron absently brought a hand to his abdomen where at times it still felt raw, despite it healing so well.

'Why would Martha leave all this lying around? Unless someone came snooping.' Theron stopped, his heart nearly stopping too. 'Shit. Lorenzo.'

He turned and ran out, Barry at his heels.

'They're walking into a trap! We have to get to that club *now!*'

Conor stood on the roof, the wind billowing his hood. The beauty of the sparkling snow did nothing to ease the heaviness on Conor's chest. On the outside, he seemed as calm as ever, but on the inside, his heart was racing. Never had he done anything so daring, had *dared* anything so reckless. Of course, the plan could fall through and his quarry could never show up.

A gust of wind made Conor shiver. He folded the flaps of his leather gloves over each finger to shield them from the cold.

Light pitter-patter of feet and the soft scrunching of snow told Conor that the acrobat assassin had arrived. He turned to face his opponent. She was clad in a tight-fitting jumpsuit with a headpiece that covered most of her neck and cheeks.

'You showed up.'

'With a challenge like that . . .' She gestured to Conor's face and then tapped her ear. 'I know you're not alone.' She pointed at the floor of the roof.

Conor took his earpiece out of his left ear and tossed it on the ground towards Marie, the ice helping it slide. She walked to it and crushed it with her heel.

'We travel roof-to-roof to where no one can find us. Then we hash things out.'

'Sounds fair.'

Marie took a running sprint and leapt gracefully over the gap, like a true ballerina. Conor let her take the lead, following a few steps behind her, jumping, landing in a crouch and rolling, and bounding along each roof until they finally stopped after ten minutes.

Conor took a brief look around, keeping a safe distance from Marie. This roof was flat, with several smoking chimneys – perhaps tied to the building's central heating – so any ice or snow had melted from it. Conor bent to peer down before taking a few steps back. 'Whoa, never realised the city looked this beautiful from up here on the roof of the Citizens Bank.'

'You have your roofs, I have mine.'

From several feet away, Marie circled Conor, keeping her long dagger sheathed.

'Since when did you become a parkour expert?' inquired Conor, turning slowly in place, his eyes always on Marie and her weapon.

'I was a ballerina before the explosion.'

'Wow, literal ballerina. That's why you're so graceful.'

'I didn't come here for praise,' Marie bit back. 'But thanks . . . I guess. Small consolation. The troupe kicked me out because I'm not pretty enough to perform on the big stage.'

'That's a load of bull, and body-shaming.' Conor pointed at Marie. 'I'm gay and I can tell you're pretty.'

Marie ripped off the cagoule of her jumpsuit, exposing her burnt and scarred face and neck.

'Now tell me that without wincing at this hideous face I have to live with because *you* stole from a pawnshop.'

'Look, had I known dirty cops were involved, I might have told my client no. I'm sorry it caused you such suffering.'

Marie laughed mirthlessly. 'Yeah, right. You just want me to stop hunting you.'

'You've figured me out,' Conor said, spreading his arms out. 'That still doesn't tell me how you linked *me* to that explosion, considering I never placed any bombs, or why you want to kill me.'

Marie stopped and gaped at Conor. 'You ruined my life!' she crowed hoarsely. 'I was bent on finding who. When I learnt about Vulpis, things started piecing together.'

'Fine, but why me? Why not go after those crooks who literally caused you those burn marks?'

Marie let out a high-pitched cackle, as though Conor had said the funniest joke. 'You think I didn't?'

Conor gulped.

'I eliminated anyone I could find. My multiple name changes are because of those mobsters coming after me, but they never saw my face, so they never knew who their assassin was.' She sighed dramatically. 'I could never find who the crooked cop was, but I might someday find them. So now,' she mock-pouted, 'the only one left to kill is you, Vulpis.'

In one swift motion, Marie unsheathed her dagger, somersaulting towards Conor and tracing an arc in the air with the blade.

Conor ducked, grabbing hold of his gun and pulling the safety. He rolled out of the way, predicting her manoeuvre and recognising it as the one that had landed his future husband in hospital. Marie landed behind Conor who spun around.

Conor shot.

Marie froze as blood spilled from her chest.

For a brief moment, Conor wondered if he had shot too soon. He hadn't wanted to take any chances, and up here, alone with Marie, he needed to save his life. Self-defence. *I'm not a killer,* he told himself. But the guilt of ending a life, the fear of what that made him, sent a jolt to his gut.

Marie coughed up blood, bringing her hand to her chest.

'Well played, Vulpis.'

She collapsed, dropping her dagger. Conor ran to her and caught her before she hit the ground. His emotions overwhelmed him.

'I'm sorry,' he whispered. Conor wished he'd shot to injure instead.

Marie's head lolled back and her body went limp in Conor's arms. Conor gently placed her on the ground.

'It always starts with one, and then another, and another.'

Conor's head shot up to find Lorenzo approaching from the security staircase, gun raised and trained on Conor. His drawl was condescending and mocking.

'And then the kills become easier, you start to be numb to them.'

Conor slowly rose, a trembling hand gripping his pistol, keeping it aloft.

Lorenzo stopped several feet away. 'Until one day, you *need* to kill, and doing so, you just know, will bring you' – he stretched the word – '*satisfaction.*'

'How did you find me?'

'It was easy enough.'

Conor raised his gun, holding his wrist with his other hand to steady his hold.

'That blast killed many. It ruined many more lives. I wonder what the deceased's families think of Vulpis.'

Conor hadn't thought of that. 'I know it doesn't make up for everything, but I could start a charity, make a public apology. Tell me, what do I need to do to make this right?'

Lorenzo's face contorted in disdain. 'You need to die!'

'Hands above your head, Lorenzo!' came a shout. Then a seethe. 'Or I *swear*— I will shoot you dead.'

'Theron!' Panic gripped Conor, his eyes going wide as the blood drained from his face.

Theron scurried onto the roof, his gun pointed at Lorenzo.

'Put the gun down now, Lorenzo! I won't ask you again.' Theron pulled his pistol's hammer back.

'Loverboy has to do it first.'

'Okay, I will. I'll put my gun down.' Conor started crouching very slowly, his palms open.

'Conor, what are you doing?'

Conor met Theron's gaze. 'I need you to trust me.'

Conor placed the gun on the ground and slowly rose.

'You know,' Lorenzo chuckled, 'I never miss a shot. That night, I shot to injure you because I still thought *this idiot* was going after you and would put you behind bars.' He growled through clenched teeth, '*I* wanted to be the one to hunt Vulpis! But once Barry left, it just *had* to go to Theron.' He spat on the ground. 'Should've shot to kill that night. My personal vengeance would have finally been done.'

'Lorenzo?' Theron warned through his teeth. 'Gun. Down. Now!'

Lorenzo chuckled. 'All right, all right. So bossy. He like that with you, Vulpis?' Lorenzo slowly crouched.

Conor was so scared Lorenzo would shoot Theron.

As Lorenzo placed his gun on the ground, he tilted it up with a deft flick – and fired.

# Chapter 8

It felt like time and Theron's life had stopped.

'Conor!!!' Theron screamed.

Theron shot Lorenzo in the heart, killing him instantly before running to Conor. The thief grunted, bringing his hands to his chest as blood drenched his clothes and spilled onto his hands. Then his eyes rolled to the back of his head. He collapsed.

Theron caught Conor just as he was hitting the ground. Theron fell to his knees, cradling Conor in his arms, sobbing and wailing his sorrow.

'Conor, darling, please stay with me.' Theron saw that Conor was still breathing. 'Please, I need you!'

Theron began to rock in place, cupping Conor's face. His voice was a mix of coughed sobs and tearful whispers. 'Please, my love, I need you. I need you in my life. You're the love of my life. I can't do this without you. Vulpis is my purpose. *You're* my purpose.' Theron wailed, 'Conor, darling, please!'

Conor opened his eyes, crying out in pain.

'Conor!' cried Theron. 'Stay with me, okay? We're going to get through this.'

Conor reached a hand up to Theron. He spoke feebly. 'I'm not dying without marrying you.'

Theron's tears fell onto Conor's face as he nodded over him, rocking Conor. The blood just kept spilling. 'You'll survive – we're going to make sure you do.' His voice cracked. 'I'm not letting you die.'

'Babe, Theron, I am surviving.' His voice had more strength this time. It almost sounded like he was apologising.

Martha ran onto the scene and secured the bodies quickly. 'All clear!' she shouted. Then she nodded to Conor. 'Good work.'

Theron glanced from Conor to Martha. 'I don't understand.'

Conor sat up and lifted his shirt, showing the blood packs and contraptions above a bulletproof vest lined with a metal padding akin to armour beneath it that told Theron they had planned for a potential stabbing attempt too.

Theron sobbed a high-pitched one and put a hand to his mouth.

Conor cupped Theron's face. 'I am so sorry we couldn't tell you. If this was a trap, we needed to catch Lorenzo off guard. We needed him to think he could kill me. And if he shot me, it needed to look legit. You weren't supposed to be on the scene. I'm so sorry you witnessed that.'

Theron kissed Conor aggressively, claiming his mouth and sobbing loudly. Then he leaned his forehead on Conor's and wept until they had to leave the scene.

* * *

Theron balled his hands into fits, needing to punch something. He glared at Martha and seethed through clenched teeth. 'Why the hell did you never tell me this plan? Conor could have gotten killed.'

'It was last minute. I'm sorry. I put this together and he agreed.'

'It was reckless!' Theron argued over Martha.

Martha raised her voice to be heard. 'We needed to work fast. And set the trap. We were banking on Lorenzo shooting him in the heart.'

'Cut the wind right out of me, I passed out.'

'And if he had shot him in the head? What then?' Theron leaned forward, glaring, wanting Martha to know he could punch her right now, uncaring of the consequences. 'Conor could have died!'

'Lorenzo was never a headshot guy.' Martha inclined her head forward. 'It was a gamble we were willing to take.'

'Never – *ever* –' shouted Theron before lowering his voice to a dangerous threat, 'gamble my future husband's life again. Do you hear me?'

'Understood.'

* * *

Theron was quiet the whole way home.

Conor felt pang after pang of worry and guilt. 'I am so sorry, Theron.'

Theron never responded.

The plan had been to lure Marie out and lure Lorenzo by leaving files out in plain view. Lorenzo had grabbed an extra earpiece – the whole unit was over-hearing. Vulpis had two earpieces in, having suspected Marie would have him remove the only one she thought he had.

Conor had been well-padded for both types of injury, gunshot and stabbing. He hadn't expected to lose consciousness, but it made it look more legit. His brain hadn't registered Theron killing Lorenzo.

Be that as it may, it didn't go unnoticed to Conor that not only had Theron shot instantly to protect him the minute Lorenzo had taken his shot, but he had killed – for the second time in his life, and this time, he had killed for Conor.

Theron had followed Lorenzo, having tracked him easily after arriving at the club and seeing Lorenzo take off in his car. His hunch had been to follow the man. Theron had shouted about that on their way to the station.

Now Barry had stayed behind at H.Q. to catch up with Martha after Theron and Conor left for home.

Theron's mouth was pressed closed, jaw tight, eyes on the road, his grip on the steering wheel so tight his knuckles were white. It tore Conor apart that Theron was so angry.

Conor and Martha had not planned for Theron at all. Conor felt guilty and angry too. Theron could have been injured again or killed this time. It was all too much, the emotions, the silence. Conor pressed a hand to his mouth, looking out the window, and squinted as tears trickled down his face.

When they walked through the door, Theron slammed it shut. He stood there for only a heartbeat. Then he grabbed Conor by the collar and pinned him against the wall hard. He pressed himself to Conor and claimed his lips, opening his mouth and sobbing as his tongue jabbed aggressively into Conor's mouth.

Conor gasped, feeling Theron's desperation, feeling his need – both their need for each other.

Theron pulled away to catch his breath, weeping.

'Babe, Theron.'

'I need to make love to you. I just need you right now!'

'I need you too.'

Theron sobbed back to Conor's lips, and after a tearful culmination, the two held each other in bed as Theron continued to weep in Conor's arms.

When Theron had calmed and when Conor too had stopped shedding tears, Conor gently stroked Theron's face with the back of his fingers.

'We've been through a lot. But we're safe now. I'm—'

'Stop apologising, Conor.' Theron's tone was gentle despite his words. 'I understand why you did it, why you couldn't tell me. I just . . . Never again. We do things together from now on and . . .' He sighed. He clenched his teeth, speaking through them. 'I just want to take that probation contract and rip it! And then we can be free to do what we want – together.'

'Who's being reckless now? We do that and we both become wanted criminals. We need to see my probation through to the end.'

'Who's being a stickler now?'

Conor took Theron's face in his hands. 'Babe, let's focus on getting married. Then we can focus on finishing my probation, and then we can assess what we want to do. We'll be free from any contracts, any legal entanglements. We can do what we want without anyone hounding us, just you and me, thief and hunter together.'

Conor kissed Theron gently. It was nice to be tender after the intensity of earlier.

'Okay,' Theron said softly.

* * *

So that's what they did, they focused on their wedding.

There were still some unanswered questions regarding the crooked cop who had orchestrated the events that had led to the bomb at that pawnshop. It was unnerving, to say the least, that this person was still out there, potentially keeping an eye on Vulpis. Nevertheless, there was nothing either Theron or Conor could do about it right now without knowing this cop's identity.

Instead, Conor went to the families of the people who had died in that explosion, to offer to make amends in whatever way he could. None blamed him. Yet his visits gave them a sense of closure.

Theron and Conor married mid-summer on the roof of a grand cathedral – a flat part of the roof – with only a few friends and family members present. In his vows, Theron claimed conquering his fear of heights so that their love would endure anything life threw at them, because it knew no bounds.

They giggled at their declarations, they wept at their intensity. Even Martha cried, and Theron had never seen her cry in all his years of knowing her.

Conor continued his probation, taking on legit jobs or ensuring they were made legit. Conor considered getting in touch with his parents now that he was married – married to the friend his parents had always adored, no less – but he was not ready to confront them yet, whatever confronting them entailed.

Eventually, Theron and Conor fell into a comfortable routine, and were now ready to make plans for the next stage of their married lives, two years later.

* * *

Theron and Conor marched into Martha's office, hand in hand. The probation on Vulpis had lifted, and the two husbands knew exactly what they wanted to do now.

'Congratulations, Vulpis.' Martha smiled, taking a step towards the two husbands. 'I'd like to offer you both a promotion.'

Theron glanced at Conor. 'Actually.' Theron un-clipped his pistol and racked the slide to show the empty chamber. He placed the pistol on Martha's desk. Conor did the same. Then both men placed their badges on her desk.

Martha put her hands on her hips. 'You're going independent, aren't you?'

'Something like that, but we won't be far. Just . . . we'll be doing simpler jobs. Less dangerous.'

Martha arched an eyebrow. 'Less reckless?'

Theron chuckled as Conor grinned. Theron hugged Conor's arm.

'Married to this guy? No chance. But we're going to start a Private Investigation firm. The non-dangerous kind.'

'You know you're going to get wives wanting to know if their husbands are cheating.'

Conor laughed. 'Everyone knows who Vulpis is now anyway. Getting married on a roof might have given our duo away, but people still need me to help them retrieve things. As a separate unit, we can still do that, and be legal, without getting into gunfights.'

Martha clicked her tongue and shook her head, her smile never faltering. She opened up her arms, closing the distance, and gave them a hug.

* * *

*One month later.*

Theron picked up the phone. Conor, leaning against the doorframe to the office in their small agency space, watched him. On the desk, Theron had placed the silly fortune-teller orb he had kept all these years that Conor had given him way back when.

'Vulpis Agency, how can I help you?'

Theron's tone was much more affable when he answered here, and Conor enjoyed the way he smiled when he did so – Conor had chided him that he should have a friendlier tone at their personal firm.

'Yes, you can e-mail the details. . . . Of course. . . . I'll discuss the details with my partner and we'll get back to you. . . . Yes, my partner is my husband. . . . Thank you! . . . Okay, thanks. Bye.'

Conor was grinning. 'You're blushing.'

Theron chuckled, stepping away from the desk. 'Uh, simple job, tracking down something forgotten at several possible locations – clubs.'

'Oooh, you taking me clubbing, babe?' Conor pushed away from the doorframe and wrapped his arms around Theron's waist. He leaned in for an enticing kiss, nibbling his husband's lower lip.

Theron hummed, smiling. 'Warming me up, darling? It's been a cold one, eh.'

Conor chuckled, seeing the blush on his husband's cheeks. 'Spring's just around the corner. It'll warm up soon.'

'Technically, March *is* Spring, and it's still cold here.'

Conor opened his mouth to object when the door opened and the bamboo bells chimed. In walked two tall Japanese men clad in business suits.

Theron and Conor stepped away from each other. 'Welcome to the Vulpis Agency. How can we help?'

Theron motioned for them to sit. The men took the two seats, and Theron and Conor sat behind their long desk.

The tallest of the two had a long face and strong jaw and cheekbones, deep grey eyes, and black hair that fell past his ears. While his complexion was mellow, the melanin in his skin gave him a neutral bronze tone, while his companion's complexion reflected more yellow tones.

'You have gained quite the reputation. Vulpis and the detective who now accompanies him.' His voice was of a tenor range when he spoke.

'Yes, I was his hunter and now, well, we're married so . . .'

'As we had surmised.' The man spoke with a mild accent; his English was excellent. 'We have a job for you, though it is a bit more high stakes than what you're used to nowadays.'

'Sorry gentlemen, but we don't do dangerous jobs anymore. Besides, that wouldn't be legal anyway, now that I am no longer with the same agency. My title legally has changed.' Theron folded his arms, leaning back.

Since starting their new firm, Theron and Conor no longer wielded guns. Theron had a taser, and Conor preferred to only have his tools – his slingshot and his card-knife. Even if Theron still had a gun licence, he was done with that.

'The job wouldn't be here.' The man leaned forward, clasping his hands. 'We want you to come help us retrieve something in Osaka.'

Theron and Conor both took a quick beat.

'Japan?' gaped Theron. 'You want us to fly out to Japan? Who are you?'

Conor clocked the pistol at the man's belt as he placed a hand on his hip, suavely flapping open his jacket – he was purposely showing them he was armed.

'We are *Yakuza.*'

Theron and Conor whipped their heads to each other and simultaneously said, 'Japanese mafia!'

'You are knowledgeable.'

Theron steepled his fingers. 'Listen, we appreciate you considering us for this job. We don't do anything dangerous anymore. We're done with that.'

The other mobster slapped an image on the desk.

Theron scowled. 'What's this?'

'This is an item I retrieved for a client.' said Conor. He recognised the clip drive immediately. 'It was legit stolen from them.'

An Asian man had approached Conor, claiming to represent a client, and had brought the receipts Conor needed to prove the clip drive belonged to their organisation, whatever that was. At the time, Conor thought nothing more of it. Now he realised he must have been dealing with mobsters who were this Yakuza man's rivals.

'Except that person first stole what belonged to *me.* Before we could track our quarry down here, he moved back to Osaka and is conducting his business there again. We want you to help us retrieve this clip drive from this person.'

'Wait, you expect us to agree to go to Japan with you for this?' Theron pointed at the Yakuza, 'Why can't *you* get it yourselves? You seem well resourced.'

'Our faces are too recognisable, Mister Morin, as I'm certain you understand. Plus, entering the facility requires more . . . unique skills, the kind of which Vulpis possesses.'

Conor exhaled slowly through his nose, still staring at the image. 'I'm sorry. I can't help you.'

'We're not asking.' The man placed his hand on his pistol, while the other unclipped a taser.

Conor clenched his jaw and swallowed hard, exchanging a furtive glance with Theron.

'Now, you can either come with us willingly and enjoy the luxuries of my private jet. Or . . . we can take you by force.'

*To be continued.*

<u>THANK YOU SO MUCH FOR READING</u>

*If you enjoyed this story,*
*please consider taking a few moments*
*to write a review on Amazon or Goodreads.*
*It would mean so much.*


*Thank you.*

Please enjoy this passage from

# The Thief & His Hunter

Book 3

# CHAPTER 1

*Present Moment.*

Theron and Conor sat in the private jet as it flew above the world – destination: Osaka, Japan.

Theron harrumphed, crossing his arms. The seats were luxurious, everything was above and beyond what First Class could ever offer, and yet, the fact that they sat facing two armed mafia men prevented Theron from enjoying the flight.

Conor, who sat beside him, was scrolling through images on Theron's phone – the thief, as per, had left his at home. 'Oh, look, there she is looking like the cutie she is.'

'Mmhmm,' Theron answered absent-mindedly, as he glowered at his . . . What, captors? They weren't bound, but . . .

'Babe, you're not even looking.'

'Huh?' Theron turned his head to Conor.

The thief waved the phone about. 'Fidelis, all adorable, playing with Barry.'

'Sorry if I can't appreciate it when we're literally sitting in front of two mobsters who forced us on this plane with them.'

Conor sighed. He glanced at the leader. 'Honestly, I appreciate you letting me stop by home to grab my gear and say a temporary goodbye to my dog.'

The man with the longer face, who seemed to be in charge, smirked, looking entertained. 'I did not realise Vulpis had so many copies of his armour.'

'Ooh, armour. Did you hear that, babe?' Conor nudged Theron with his shoulder.

'How are you this excitable?'

'Theron. The guy put his hand on his gun. Neither of them ever actually threatened us at gunpoint.'

The man had certainly made his point and gotten their 'cooperation.' And yet, he *had* allowed them to stop by home. Still, they were mobsters, and that made them lawbreakers.

Theron narrowed his eyes. 'Not even halfway there and you're suffering from Stockholm syndrome.'

Conor rolled his eyes. 'I am making the best of our situation.'

'That's because you're reckless. *I* prefer to remain cautious.'

'As do we.' Their host looked more than amused. 'Do keep in mind that we are aware your dogsitter is your former detective partner, Mister Morin, and that we have long since flown out of American air. Anything he may relay to your former boss will do nothing to change your situation or save you from it.'

Theron just scowled harder in response.

Conor put the phone away. 'Maybe it would help if you told us your names, now that we are in the air, away from home. I need to build trust with my clients.'

'Of course. I would also like to establish trust with you, as well as establish the finer details of our agreement.'

'Agreement is a generous word,' Theron muttered under his breath.

'While we will not be paying you until the job is complete,' their Japanese host went on, 'you will be lodged, and equipped with the necessary.'

'You mean guns.' Theron huffed and sighed.

'All right.' The man stood and bowed curtly from the waist. Theron recognised the show of respect. The Japanese man sat back down. 'Kiyoshi Tachibana. Yakuza leader of Tachibana Clan in the Osaka prefecture.' He pointed his thumb at his compatriot. 'And my bodyguard and trusted friend, Aritomo-san.'

Theron nodded in acknowledgement, while Conor held out his hand.

'Vulpis. You can call me Conor.'

They shook hands.

'I can't believe you're actually enjoying yourself,' muttered Theron. 'Honestly, you're so reckless.'

'Stickler,' Conor muttered back without even looking at Theron.

Kiyoshi chuckled.

'So . . . there's something I've been trying to make sense of since we took flight,' began Conor, adopting a comfortable pose in his seat. 'Because you said the guy with the clip drive first took something from you.' Conor pointed behind him. 'That clip drive had a receipt. From a long time ago. Honestly, I was surprised his people still had his receipt.'

'It is not the clip drive that belongs to us.'

'What!' exclaimed Theron.

'But what it contains.'

'Wait,' said Conor. 'Ohhh, so the clip drive has *information* that's yours.'

'You never investigated the drive?' Kiyoshi inquired, quirking an eyebrow.

'I don't pry,' replied Conor. 'But a drive with info on enemy mobsters . . . well, I guess that explains his urgency to have it retrieved.'

Theron was confused. 'If he has info on you, then isn't it too late to erase that?'

'You don't understand, Mister Morin. It is not *what* is on the drive that is mine, but the information will lead to what *is*.'

'I'm not following.'

Kiyoshi stood and crossed the aisle to stare out the window at the bright sun as they flew high above the clouds. The warm light cast an orange glow on his bronze face.

'I am searching for a woman. The information on the drive will lead me to her.'

'How do you know this?' asked Conor.

Kiyoshi, his back to them, explained. 'The man, Shibuya, took something from me a long time ago, and that clip drive is the key to finding . . . her. Shibuya is a rival of the Yakuza and leads a mafia called *Nesshiin'na Kōkan* – Diligent Exchange.' Kiyoshi balled his hands into fists and his voice grew rough. 'He is a human slave trafficker.'

Something hit Theron in the pit of his stomach. 'Shit. And Shibuya took that woman from you.' He raised his voice. 'Oh my god, you're into human slave trafficking too, aren't you?'

Kiyoshi looked back over his shoulder. 'Think what you want, Mister Morin. I will not waste my breath on meaningless drivel or arguments.'

'Wait,' Conor said gently. He placed his hand on Theron's arm. 'I don't think that's what it is.' He looked up at Kiyoshi. 'Who is this woman to you?'

Kiyoshi faced them anew, his face deceiving his grief. 'She is my sister.'

Theron's stomach clenched, and the reality of it all hit him like a punch in the gut. 'Shit. I'm sorry.'

Theron had misjudged the situation. Sure, he had his judgements – and reservations – but this man, despite being a mafia boss in his prefecture, was looking for his sister. And the way he felt about what Shibuya did for a living told Theron that Kiyoshi had enough of a conscience to be against acts as vile as human slave trafficking.

Kiyoshi returned to his seat. He folded a leg, resting his ankle on his knee. 'The *Nesshïn'na Kōkan* attacked the Yakuza one night and took Azumi-san, my sister, from us. Just like they took many girls from many regions. That is the night they killed my father.'

Kiyoshi's eyes grew distant for a moment, as though he were reliving the events of that night.

'I am the eldest of three children. I was too young to take over from my father then. My brother and I have been searching for my sister ever since. It has been . . . twenty years. She was 13. I was 15.'

Theron and Conor exchanged a glance, smiling in sympathy.

'Yeah, we know what it's like to be searching for someone, sort of, for that long,' Conor said gently. 'Not the same, of course, but . . .'

'Then you understand the . . .' Kiyoshi searched for the word. He put a hand to the centre of his chest.

'Yeah, it grips you and . . . consumes you,' said Conor.

'That is why I need your services, Vulpis.'

Conor nodded slowly. 'So the clip drive must contain records of all the girls this guy has been trafficking over the years, where they were last, and if—' He stopped abruptly. 'Sorry.'

'If they were ever sold or killed,' completed Kiyoshi. He sighed, leaning back, head resting against the head-rest as he gazed towards the far window.

'I'll get that clip drive,' asserted Conor. 'And we'll find your sister.'

Kiyoshi offered him a mild smile in thanks before the four men fell silent.

# The Thief & His Hunter

## Book 3

*Look for it in bookstores September 2025.*

<u>Also By</u>

Also Written by Eidahs

*Sanguine Sincerity*
*(https://binkyproductions.com/Tenebrarum)*

*The Thief and His Hunter Book 1*
*(https://binkyproductions.com/TheThiefandHisHunter)*

*Like Father, Not Like Sons*
*Legacy Takedown*
*Of Sullied Dreams and Beaten Hearts*
*Butchery At the Debauchery*
*Serendipitous Tribulation*
*Turbulent Justice*
*(https://binkyproductions.com/shortstories)*

*You will find more books*
*published by Binky Ink at:*
*https://binkyproductions.com/books*

# About the Author

Eidahs is a pseudonym for all mature written works, from thrillers to erotic romance. Eidahs in pronunciation sounds elven in nature, which is why she chose it, to tap into her love of fantasy, a genre that couples well with super-natural and preternatural, dark fantasy, and romance.

Eidahs is also the nickname 'Shadie' backwards, representing the shadow self, innermost desires, and a spectrum of emotions, most notably, passion, sorrow, rage, and delight, which Eidahs loves to incorporate in her writing. Enticing readers and evoking the characters' emotions when she writes has guided her inspiration to spell many short stories on Medium and a series of books under this pen name.

*Connect with Binky Ink:*

WordPress Website & Blog
     https://binkyproductions.com/binkyinkwriting
Medium – Main Profile
     https://medium.com/@BinkyInkWriting
X (Twitter) https://twitter.com/binkyinkwriting
Inkitt https://inkitt.com/eidahs